LAUREN GRABOIS

LIFE

ILLUSTRATED BY
DEVIN HUNT

The
Be
Books

www.TheBEbooks.com

I hope that you enjoy this book and the fun activities that follow after. If you come up with a great activity that promotes kindness, positivity, and love, and you want to share it with me, you can email your ideas to **lauren@thebebooks.com** or find me on social media **@thebebooks**!

You can follow my page for positive posts, updates on book giveaways, and new book releases.

I would love to share your beautiful creations with others. You can have your parents or teachers post them on social media and tag **@thebebooks**. Make sure to use **#thebebooks** and **#laurengraboisfischer** in your posts.

Copyright ©2020, 2021 The BE Books Inc.
All Rights Reserved,
Published by The BE Books

No part of this book may be reproduced or transmitted in any form or by any means, electronic or mechanical, including photocopying or recording without written permission from the publisher.

Softcover - ISBN: 978-0-9862532-7-0
Hardcover - ISBN: 978-1-7333026-4-7

www.TheBEbooks.com
@theBEbooks

Printed in the USA
Signature Book Printing, www.sbpbooks.com

Dedication Page

This book was inspired by the deep and meaningful relationship between my son and my grandfather, Joseph. I will never forget the day that my grandpa held my son for the first time. That love, that moment, will be with me forever.

This book is dedicated to my father-in-law, Laszlo. Laszlo, a Holocaust survivor, lost his three-week battle with COVID on April 5, 2020. Although you were a man of 81 years, you were the perfect example that age is just a number. Your energy, love, dedication, commitment, and loyalty will forever be missed, and we will be forever grateful for having you in our lives. You were Isaac's best friend and held such an important place in his heart. Thank you for always showing up and being here for us all. Thank you for the love and guidance which you always had time to give. Thank you for being the best father in the world. We love you to heaven and back.

I want to dedicate this book to the families who have lost a loved one so suddenly due to COVID-19. May their memories be a blessing, and may you live your life in honor of them. They would want you to be present and happy.

A great grandson sat quietly next to his great grandfather.

He stared at him wondering for quite some time.

Then with a bit of courage he asked,

"What is it like to be old?"

His great grandfather sat
up tall in his chair and
began to answer,

"Well...

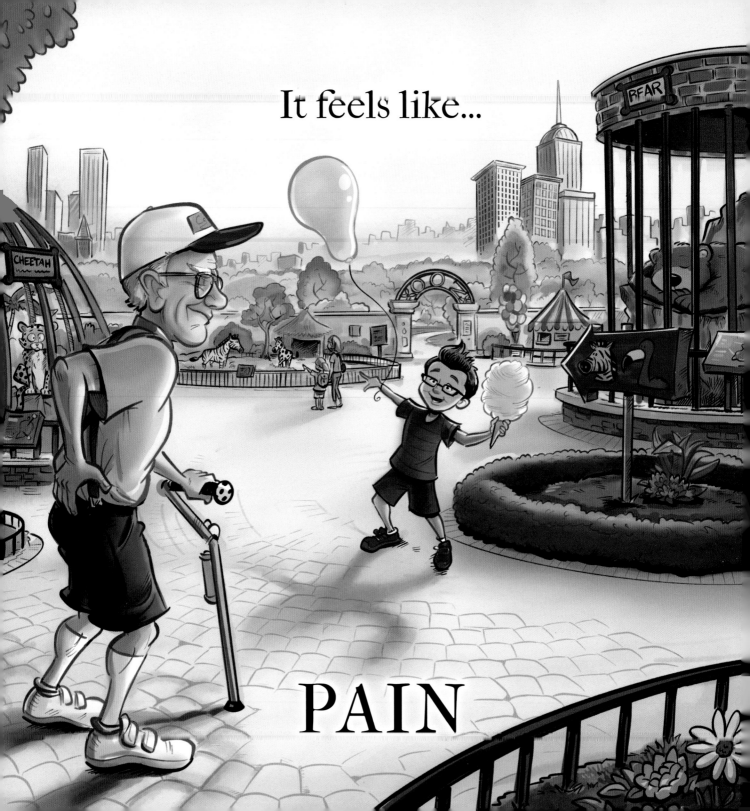

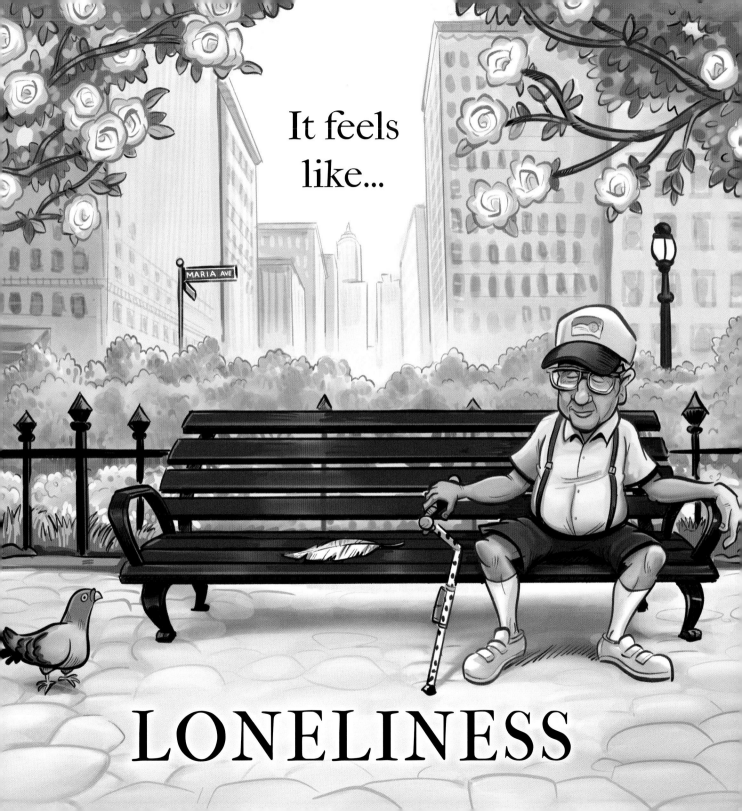

It feels like...

FUN

And the Great Grandfather continued...

"Being old is not so bad.
What is it like to be young?"

The great grandson replied,

"Well...

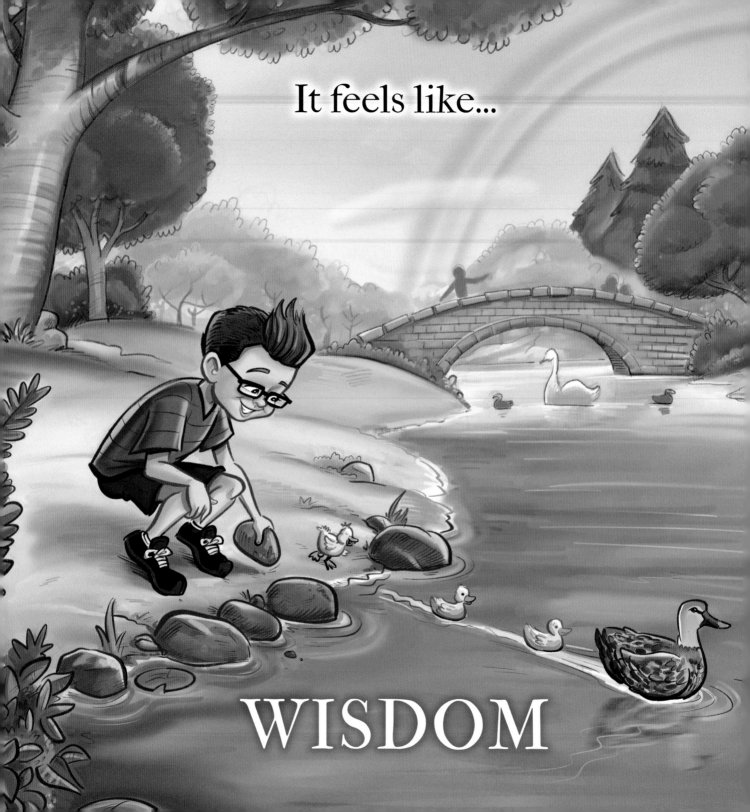

It feels like...

FAMILY

It feels
like...

LOVE

It feels like...

FUN

It feels like...

KNOWLEDGE

It feels like...

LAUGHTER

The little boy continued, "Being young isn't so bad."
The two hugged and laughed.

The little boy looked at his great
grandpa and said, "Isn't life great?"

And his great grandpa looked at him and smiled.

"It sure is."

INSPIRATION & DISCUSSION

Sit and relax with someone you love. Ask each other the questions below. It is always wonderful to sit and talk with your family and friends.

- What is your favorite thing to be grateful for?

- Who do you enjoy spending time with?

- Ask your parents about your grandparents.
  Find out where they were born. Find out who their parents were.
  It is a beautiful thing to know where you come from.

- When do you feel at peace? What calms you down?

- What does "fun" look like for you?

- Everyone gets scared sometimes. What do you do to feel safe?
  How can your loved ones help you when you are feeling uncertain?

- What do you like to do with your family? Where is your favorite place to visit?

- When were you brave? Share your story with a friend or loved one.

- Do you love to laugh? What is your favorite joke? How do you get your parents to laugh?

- Do you enjoy listening to music? Do you play a musical instrument? Have you always
  wanted to learn one?

- What is your favorite page in this book? Why?

ACTIVITY PAGES

A Gratitude List

Gratitude will create your attitude. Remember this always! Every morning when you wake up, think of five to ten things that you are grateful for. It can be anything from the smallest thing to the biggest thing. Below are some examples:

• I am grateful for waking up.

• I am grateful for my parents.

• I am grateful for my siblings.

• I am grateful that I can share my ideas.

• I am grateful that I can bike ride.

• I am grateful for the beautiful day outside.

Now it is your turn. Find someone that you love and share five to ten things that you are grateful for. If no one is around, go sit in front of your mirror and talk to your very best friend, YOU! Your reflection will be very happy to listen.

Kind Self-Talk

We would not dare speak unkindly to someone who we love. We watch what we say as to not hurt others' feelings. But sometimes we do not hear how we speak to ourselves. Sometimes we are unaware of our own inner dialogue in our heads. This activity is so important because our relationship with ourselves is the most important relationship that you will have in your life. Be your own best friend. Speak kindly and do things that you love. Find time to paint the picture that you've always wanted to paint. Find time to color and swim and laugh and smile. And most importantly, find the time to speak to your reflection. Look in the mirror and say, "I love you," at least once a day.

Speak kindly to yourself by using **"I am…"** and **"I can…"** statements. For example: I am kind. I am beautiful. I am happy. I am generous. I am a good friend. I am healthy. I am going to be okay. I can do anything. I can help my sister. I can get an A.

Now it is your turn:

I am _____

I am _____

I am _____

I am _____

I am _____

I can _____

Kindness Rocks

Collect rocks from your backyard or purchase some online. Take out paint and markers. It is fun to paint the rocks and then let them dry. Once dry, use your markers to write positive quotes and sayings on them. Go on a walk with your family and leave the rocks in your community or on your block. Let others find them. This will affect their day in a positive way, and it will make you feel good too. When you help others, it lights up your life as well.

Breathe

Our breath is a powerful thing. We can connect to our inner self by being still and relaxing. When we feel like we are overwhelmed or upset, we need it most. So find a safe place in your house, and create a "mindful" spot where you can always go to. Take a seat and breathe. Close your eyes and focus on counting your breaths. Breathe in, 1, 2, 3, breathe out, 1, 2, 3. Repeat this as many times as you need to feel calm and relaxed and whole. Taking the time to breathe and listen to your inner voice is the most powerful way to heal your mind. Take control by relaxing and being present in this moment.

Exercise

Exercise comes in all types and forms. Get your heart rate up, and you will be healthier in body and mind. There is no one way to exercise. Play loud music and dance away. Go on a nightly walk with your family. Go outside and swim in your pool. Do jumping jacks or jump rope. Buy a hula-hoop and have a contest with a family member to see who can go the longest. Jump on a trampoline. Ride your bike.

- **How do you like to exercise?**

- **What is your favorite way to burn some energy?**

- **How many jumping jacks can you do?**

- **How many sit-ups can you do?**

How Will You Change the World?

Here are some things to think about. Ask your parent(s), teacher(s), or sibling(s) to go over these with you. Share your answers.

What will I do to make a positive change in our world?

How can I be kind to others?

What is something that I love and appreciate?

How can I make someone smile?

How can I make today count? What is my purpose today?

Finish the sentences:

I love life because _____

I will heal the world by _____

I make myself happy by _____

I make others smile when _____

I am important because _____

Rules to Live By For A Beautiful Life

1. Wake up grateful each and every single day.

2. Speak kind words to yourself and to others.

3. Be patient with yourself and others.

4. Find your purpose in each day and live with meaning.

5. Give back to others and the world.

6. Be true to yourself and stand up for what you believe in.

7. Dream big and set attainable goals all while still challenging yourself.

8. Have faith in the process of life and believe that all will be okay.

9. Make sure to laugh every single day.

10. Value yourself, your family, and friends.

11. Radiate happiness and love onto others and the world.

12. Inspire others.

13. NEVER give up.

14. You are more than enough.

The Inspiration Behind This Book

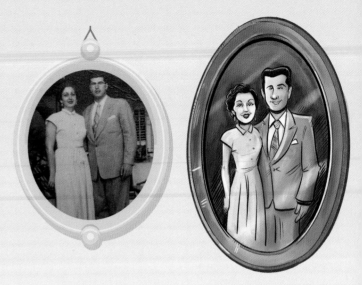

I was sitting and thinking about the beauty of life one day. I was feeling grateful for my family and for the connection that my son and my grandfather had. I watched as they hugged and talked to each other. How lucky I felt that my son was able to have his 91 year old great grandfather in his life. My children have both been blessed with the love, attention, and dedication that only a grandparent can give. They have been blessed to have grandparents who enrich their lives and who are part of their day-to-day growth. My son and daughter are extremely close to all of their grandparents and even their two great grandparents.

As I was pondering the thought about life, it occurred to me that no matter the age, life is all about perspective. Your *Age* is just a number. *Beauty* truly lies in the eyes of the beholder. *Gratitude* is something that we choose. *Fear* is something that everyone has to face and bravery is something that we are all capable of. *Wisdom* comes from that inner voice. *Music* heals the soul no matter your age. *Peace* is felt from within. And *love* is what keeps us all here. I felt the power in my thoughts and knew that a new book had to be born. I knew that I needed to share the wisdom of LIFE with the world.

This book was created based on real events, real people, and real love.

LIFE is beautiful.

"Life" Has Changed - April 2020 | The Author's Perspective - For the Parents

Dear Parents,

The irony is that I now sit here writing this letter to you. Our "life" and our world as we know it has changed. We are experiencing something that we never could have imagined and somehow we are still having difficulty absorbing the "new normal." The day-to-day routines that we thought were so important, just four weeks ago, are now a distant memory. And the family who we are blessed to have, they are all spread out across the world. Video chats have become the new normal, and gratitude is something that we are all holding onto tightly. Life as we know it, changed right in front of our eyes.

This book, *"Life"*, has been in the works for a year and a half. I have poured my heart and soul directly into it, as it holds so much of my life in it. As it is coming together, "real life" is simultaneously happening. There have been many changes, both positive and negative, in the world and in my world. Most recently, due to COVID-19, all of our lives have been put on pause. The activities that had become so important and made up our daily routines, are now a faded memory as we learn to entertain ourselves at home. Lives are being lost due to this horrible illness that is spreading much too quickly.

I am at a loss for words trying to express how this illness hit closer to home than we could have imagined. My husband lost his dear father, who was his best friend, to this horrible illness. My children lost their "Papi," and my mother-in-law lost her Superman and husband of 54 years. There are now five grandchildren missing their grandfather and two children missing their father. The unimaginable has happened.

You may be asking, "Why bring up COVID-19 in a book about life?" Throughout the last year and a half, I wanted this book to take form and become a part of each of your homes immediately. I felt it so important to remind others about the importance of family and about how our perspectives can affect our lives. For some unknown reason, the universe kept postponing my completion of this book. As each picture slowly came to life, the deep meaning put into each illustration became even more important than it had been during the idea phase of this book. My grandfather was diagnosed with cancer, and most recently, my father-in-law, Laszlo, passed away from his three week battle with COVID-19. So I refer back to the question that I think everyone is asking, "Why? Why bring up a topic that is causing so much harm?" I bring it up for a few reasons. For the first time ever, everyone in this world is actually on the same page. We are all dealing with the loss of our normal lives.

We are all mourning the changes of our day-to-day routines. And some of us are mourning the loss of a loved one. The world is in a place that none of us are familiar with and we are all learning it together. It is our responsibility to #stayhome and to #beselfless. What one of us does on one end of the world, someone else sees the effects. This is our opportunity to be careful and safe and help others through our selfless actions. I feel it is so important that we all understand how much power that is. Let this time in our lives bring us together, and let it empower us to do the right thing. Let it wake us up from the routines that we created and create new ones. Routines that can heal our world as a whole and create a wholeness to our world. For the first time ever, we are all living our lives at the same pace. Now more than ever, we are all connected. Let's remember that. Let's use our power to make a positive change. Let's make this world a better place than it was before it all changed.

What do we do with these changes? How can we grow and learn and better ourselves? How can we use this time to become better people and contribute to society in a more positive way? Although we cannot understand the cause of an illness spreading throughout our world, and the loss of life that it is taking; we can somehow find good in everything. Choose to see that good. Choose to find the beauty in the world around you. Choose to find the wisdom inside of yourself. Choose to surrender and accept the new normal ways. After all, your perspective will shape and create your world. Spend time with that family for whom you have always felt grateful. Cuddle, hug, talk, play games, and just be there for one another. If you cannot physically be close, find a way to emotionally be there for each other. Smile at the people that you pass on your evening walks. Say hello to a stranger who may be feeling lonely in isolation. Help others. Be positive and spread happiness into the digital world. Do not contribute to the stresses and negativity. Instead, find a way to be the light that this world so desperately is seeking. Share what you have with those who may need it. If you are out shopping and see an elderly person who could use your help, take the time to help them. After all, "Life" is really about giving and receiving love, caring for one another, finding your purpose, and sharing your time with your loved ones. Life is a gift. Let's be grateful for it.

With Love, Light, and Gratitude Always,
Lauren Grabois Fischer

Life has a beautiful way of sending you just what you need.

Gramps - Your ongoing support and love for your family is admirable, and I am forever grateful for the closeness that you and I share. You have always shown a dedication to me, and you mean the world to me. I will always be your dimpled girl.

I love you forever and always.

To my second father, Laszlo - In just 11 years of being your daughter-in-law, the bond that we created will last a lifetime and for that, I am forever grateful. Thank you for going above and beyond... always. I love you.

Tying in Social Emotional Learning (SEL) with Great Picture Books

What is Social Emotional Learning? It is the way that children learn to establish and maintain friendships. It is how a child understands his or her emotions. It is creating healthy ways for children to express themselves and set goals for themselves. It is the understanding of empathy and feeling for others. It is being responsible and reliable. It is creating healthy habits. Social Emotional Learning, also known as: SEL, is one of the most important topics that we as parents and educators need to be addressing.

One thing that I absolutely LOVE is that my books are used frequently in the classroom and school environment. All of my books are used by many school counselors and teachers around the country. If you are a school counselor, teacher, or principal and you would like to get a set of **The Be Books** for your school, please send me a message. You can visit my website **www.thebebooks.com** or email **lauren@thebebooks.com**. It is so important that we show support for ALL students and offer books that can help with their emotional well-being.

The extra activity and discussion pages in the back of my books provide a healthy conversation between you and your child(ren)/student(s). These pages are geared for classrooms and homes that want to discuss positive topics and inspire children to be the positive change in their homes and in their world. These can be used as a springboard for lesson plans for teachers or questions for parents. It is a wonderful way to develop the child's vocabulary and help them to understand that their actions can change their reality.

THIS BOOK BELONGS TO:

_____

Your Name